MUPPET KIDS IN
Help! We're Lost!

By Louise Gikow

Illustrated by Tom Leigh

A GOLDEN BOOK • NEW YORK
Western Publishing Company, Inc., Racine, Wisconsin 53404

"All aboard!"
The conductor of the Beekman Express walked
down the platform, shouting to all the passengers.
"All aboard!"

Kermit's mom hugged Kermit one more time. Then she kissed Fozzie on the cheek.

"Now, you kids take care of yourselves," she said. "You have your tickets and your money, right, Fozzie?"

"Yes, Mrs. Frog." Fozzie nodded.

"Don't worry, Mom," Kermit said. "I've gone to Uncle McDermott's house lots of times."

"And I'll keep an eye on them, ma'am," added the conductor.

The conductor led Kermit and Fozzie to some seats. "Now, you kids sit tight," he told them. "I'll put your bags on the rack above you, and I'll come back and check on you whenever I can. You know the name of your stop, right?"

"Yes, sir," Kermit said. "Greenville Junction."

Kermit and Fozzie waved to Kermit's mom as the train started to pull out of the station.

"Have a good time!" she called. "And don't forget to call me and Fozzie's mother when you get there!"

"We will, Mom!" Kermit shouted back. "Good-bye!"

"Gee," Kermit said, settling back in his seat. "I love riding on trains."

"Me too," said Fozzie. "Want a banana?"

Kermit and Fozzie spent the next two hours looking out the window, talking, playing cards, and reading. Every so often, they could hear the conductor's voice calling out the stops. And he came by to say hello a few times, too.

Then it was time for lunch. Fozzie's mom had packed sandwiches and fruit and some cookies, too. Fozzie was just starting on his second banana when the conductor stopped by.

"The next stop is yours, kids," he said. "I'll take your bags down for you."

The conductor reached above their heads and took their suitcases down from the rack.

"Have we got everything?" Kermit asked.

"I think so," said Fozzie.

The train started to slow down. "Greenville! Greenville!" the conductor cried. Kermit and Fozzie walked to the end of the aisle and stood by their bags.

Suddenly, Fozzie looked around. "Teddy!" he said. "Do you have Teddy?"

"No," said Kermit. "I don't see him anywhere."

Fozzie dropped his bags and whoopee cushion and raced back to his seat. "I can't leave without him," he said frantically.

Fozzie looked around the seat and under it, but he couldn't find his teddy bear anywhere. "I have to find Teddy," he kept muttering. "I can't leave him behind."

In the meantime, everyone who had stood up when the conductor called out the stop had already gotten off the train.

"Fozzie!" Kermit shouted down the aisle. "We're going to miss our —"

And that's when the train started to move again!

"Oh, no!" Kermit cried. "Somebody stop the train!" But nobody did. Kermit watched in dismay as they pulled out of Greenville Junction.

At that moment, Fozzie poked his head up from behind the seat. "I've got Teddy!" he said happily. "We can get off now."

"No, we can't," said Kermit. "Look."

Kermit pointed to a window. Outside, the scenery was rushing by.

"We missed the stop," Fozzie cried. "What are we going to do?"

"I don't know," Kermit said, his voice shaking a little. "Maybe the conductor can tell us."

But the conductor was nowhere to be found.

"I guess we should get off at the next stop," Kermit finally said, swallowing hard.

Before he'd left home, Kermit had written down his uncle McDermott's phone number, and he was carrying a quarter, just in case. He and Fozzie got off the train and went to the nearest phone. Kermit dialed.

But the phone just rang and rang.

"We can call my mom collect," Kermit decided.

"I'll call my mom, too," Fozzie added. "I learned my phone number and the area code by heart when I was a little kid."

But Kermit's mom wasn't home, and neither was Fozzie's.

Kermit had always loved train stations. But as he looked around now, the station didn't look like a friendly place at all. He was glad he and Fozzie were together. It would be even worse if he were alone.

"Now what?" Fozzie finally said. He looked as worried as Kermit felt.

"Mom taught me what to do if I got lost," Kermit said, trying to keep calm and act grown-up. "She said to find a policeman if I was ever in trouble. So that's what I think we should do."

Kermit and Fozzie looked around for a policeman. They didn't see anyone right away. But they
did see a sign that read TICKETS.

"Gee, Kermit," Fozzie said. "My mom said that
it was safe to ask the people in the ticket booth for
help. What do you think?"

"I think that's a good idea," said Kermit.

As they picked up their bags and started to walk toward the sign, a tall man appeared out of nowhere. "You kids look lost," said the man, smiling. "Can I help you?"

Kermit looked up at the man for a second. Then he took Fozzie's arm and started to walk away as quickly as he could.

"Hey, kids!" shouted the man. "Come back."

"What should we do?" Fozzie whispered to Kermit.

"Just keep walking," Kermit told him. "My mom told me never to talk to strangers...no matter what. If I get lost, I'm supposed to find someone official to help me."

When Kermit got to the ticket booth, he looked
around. But the stranger had walked away.

A woman was standing behind the ticket window. She looked down at Kermit and Fozzie.

"Hi, kids," she said. "Can I help you?"

"You sure can," Kermit said. "We're lost."

"Don't worry," said the woman. "I'll get a policeman over here right away."

When Kermit saw the blue uniform of the policeman, he felt a *whoosh* of relief.

"Are you the kids who are lost?" the policeman asked.

"Yes, sir," said Kermit. "Me and Fozzie here. We missed our stop on the train."

"Well, let's see what we can do to help," said the policeman.

Kermit explained about his uncle McDermott and about no one's being home when they called. The first thing the policeman did was to try to call their parents again. This time, Kermit's mom answered.

"Thank heavens!" said his mom when she heard the policeman's story. "My brother McDermott just called. He was terribly worried. Just tell me where the kids are, and he'll drive over and pick them up."

After the policeman gave Kermit's mom directions, she asked to speak to Kermit.

"It was a little scary," Kermit told his mom. "But we knew all the phone numbers, and we didn't talk to strangers — just like you've always taught me."

"I'm really proud of you, Kermit," his mom replied. "You did just the right things."

"Thanks," said Kermit. "And thanks for telling me all that stuff. If you hadn't, I wouldn't have known *what* to do."

The policeman stayed with Kermit and Fozzie
until Uncle McDermott arrived at the train station.
Uncle McDermott was very glad to see them!

After Kermit and Fozzie had piled into Uncle McDermott's car, Fozzie turned to his best friend.

"Boy, Kermit," he said. "I'm really sorry for getting us into this mess. And you know what?"

"What?" Kermit asked.

"Next time we go on a trip," Fozzie said, "I'm going to leave Teddy home. He shouldn't travel without Mom and Pop until he knows *his* phone number, too!"